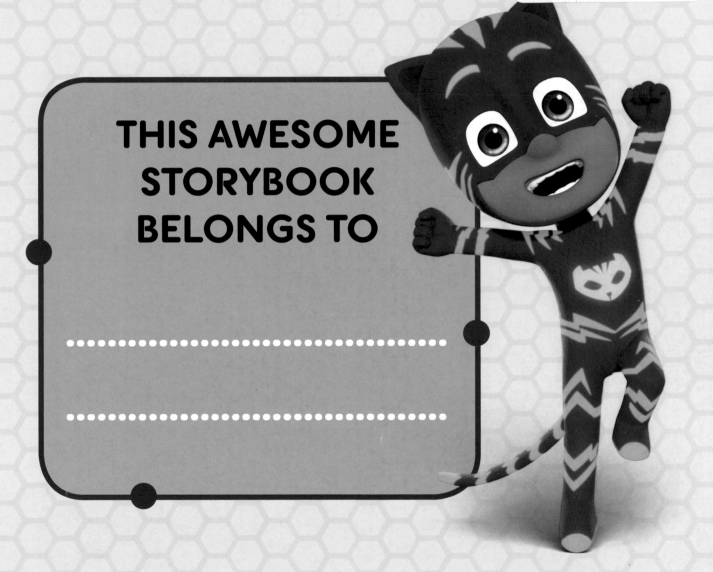

THIS AWESOME STORYBOOK BELONGS TO

....

....

Big Birthday Cake Rescue

Greg was super-excited – it was the day before his birthday!
"I've got lizard balloons and decorations," he said.
"I've even got a lizard cake!"
"That sounds so cool," laughed Amaya.

Connor stopped outside a shop window. It had an awesome
Master Fang display.
"When it's my birthday, I'm going to have a Master Fang party,"
he told his friends. Connor pretended
to karate kick, just like his hero.

"Hi-yah!"

Greg's party was going to be
at the city bookshop. He grabbed
Connor and Amaya by the arms and
pulled them along.
"Come on!" he chuckled. "It's all set up."

Greg looked inside the bookshop.

"My decorations!" he wailed.

Plants had been knocked over and bunting pulled to the floor. The box on the table was empty. Greg's lizard cake had gone!

"I'm sorry, Greg," said Connor. "Still . . . we could always go and get those cool Master Fang decorations from next door instead."

Greg spotted something on the floor.

"Ninjalino footprints!" he gasped.

"That must mean that Night Ninja has my cake."

"We'll get it back," promised Amaya.

The PJ Masks were on their way.

It was time to save Greg's birthday!

Night in the city. A brave band of heroes is ready to face fiendish villains to stop them messing with your day.

Amaya becomes
. . . OWLETTE!

Greg becomes
. . . GEKKO!

Connor becomes
. . . CATBOY!

"To the Gekko-Mobile!" shouted Gekko. "Let's get my lizard cake back!"
The heroes jumped in. The Gekko-Mobile
zoomed into the city at top speed.

Gekko spotted two Ninjalinos
running down the street. They had
his cake! The pesky pair skidded into
an alley. They pushed the cake into
a metal cage and locked it shut.

Night Ninja stepped out of the shadows.

"Come to admire my cake?" he called.

"It's not yours, it's Gekko's!" shouted Catboy.

Night Ninja clicked his fingers. A confetti bomb popped,

covering the street in party decorations.

"It's my party," he jeered, "and you're not invited!"

"Time for a party game," decided Night Ninja.

"You can't have a birthday party when it's not your birthday," yelled Gekko.

Night Ninja and his Ninjalinos sniggered. That's exactly what they had in mind!

Catboy had a challenge for Night Ninja. "I can beat you at any party game,"
he shouted, "as long as I choose what we play."
Night Ninja stamped his foot. "It's my party, so I pick the game!" he replied.

Catboy pretended to walk away in a sulk. The baddie had fallen for his plan!
"You keep Night Ninja busy," he whispered to Owlette and Gekko,
"and I'll get the cake."

Owlette stepped forward. "Gekko and I will still play," she called.
"And you will still lose!" smirked Night Ninja, holding a present in
the air. "The game is pass the parcel."

The Ninjalinos began to dance and sing.
Night Ninja tossed the present to Owlette who passed it to Gekko.
Every time it came back round to Night Ninja, he clicked his fingers
and the music stopped.

"Diddly-diddly-diddly-dee!"

"I told you I was good!" he chuckled, unwrapping layer after layer.
"Next round!"

It was a fix. Night Ninja kept on until he won the prize! The villain was so busy winning, he didn't notice Catboy creeping up towards Gekko's cake.

Night Ninja's prize was a talking mini-model of . . . Night Ninja!
He pulled a cord on its back.
"Night Ninja does everything the best!" said the toy.

"Maybe," replied a voice from above, "but we've got the cake!"
Night Ninja gasped. Catboy was making a getaway with
the lizard cake!

The PJ Masks made a dash towards the Gekko-Mobile. They would have made it, too, if Catboy hadn't spotted the party shop.

"Wow! Check out the Master Fang cake," he said. "It's the cat's whiskers!"

"Gekko doesn't want that cake," shouted Owlette. "Let's go!"

Too late. While Catboy was daydreaming, the Ninjalinos stuck a sticky splat on his back. All they had to do now was drag him straight back to Night Ninja.

Night Ninja was getting bored.

"Too bad, PJ party poopers," he yawned. "The cake's mine now. See ya!"

"No, wait!" yelled Catboy. "Let's play another game."

"We'll play musical chairs," declared Night Ninja.
Two Ninjalinos floated by holding the winner's prize –
some Master Fang balloons.

"I'll go out in the first round and get my cake," whispered Gekko.

"We'll keep Night Ninja busy," agreed Owlette. "Which means you
can't win, Catboy. The longer we all play,
the more time we get for Gekko."

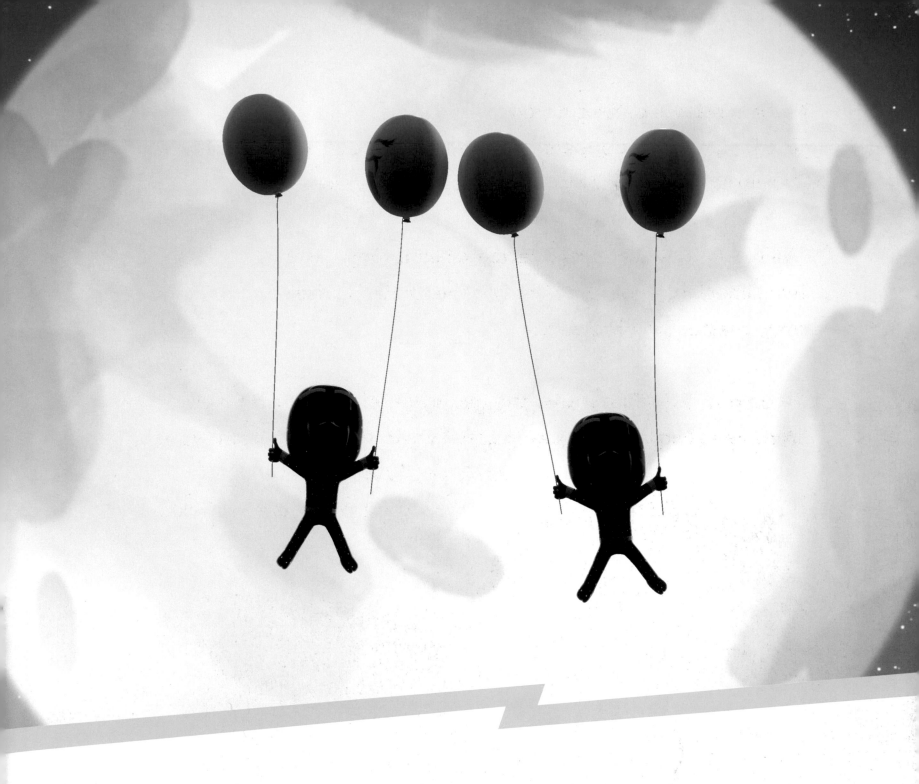

But Catboy wasn't listening.

He couldn't take his eyes off the Master Fang balloons.

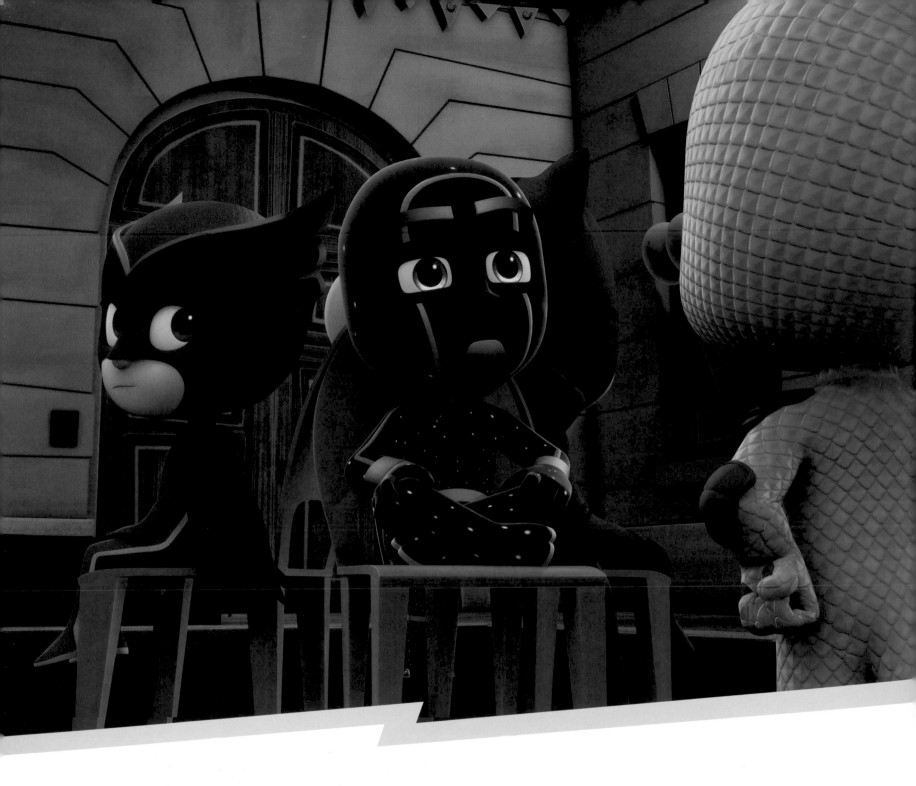

Night Ninja explained the rules. When the music stopped, everyone had to sit down . . . if they could find a seat.

"Diddly-diddly-diddly-dee!"

The Ninjalinos started to sing again. As soon as they stopped, Night Ninja scrambled to a chair. Gekko made sure he was the last one standing up. "You're out, birthday bozo!" cackled the villain.

Gekko pretended to look disappointed. When the music started again, he scuttled away. Night Ninja didn't notice him climbing up towards the cake.

"Super Lizard Grip!"

Owlette was out next.
"Catboy," she whispered.
"You need to let Night Ninja win."
Catboy gulped. Those balloons were too hard to resist. He dived on the last chair and won the game.

Night Ninja was furious.

"What?" he thundered.

Owlette blinked. Catboy had ruined their plan! Gekko made a grab for the cake, but the Ninjalinos rocked the cage, knocking it out of his hand.

"Noooo!" yelled Gekko.

Owlette swooped in just in time.

"Got it!" she cried. "Let's go!"

The PJ Masks made a run for it.

"We got the cake and these amazing Master Fang balloons!" grinned Catboy.

Gekko shook his head. "You're not listening. I'm having a lizard party."

Suddenly, Night Ninja appeared . . . holding the Master Fang cake.

"I really wanted the lizard cake," he grumbled. "Now I'm stuck with this useless one. Unless you want to swap?"

Gekko and Owlette glared at Night Ninja.
"We'd never swap!"

But Catboy couldn't take his
eyes off the Master Fang cake.
It was perfect for him! Quick as
a flash, the hero handed over
Gekko's lizard cake.

"This one is awesome!"
gushed Catboy.
"Really awesome," agreed
Night Ninja. "Especially if
you press here."
The villain flicked a switch
on the side of the Master
Fang cake. It began to
light up.

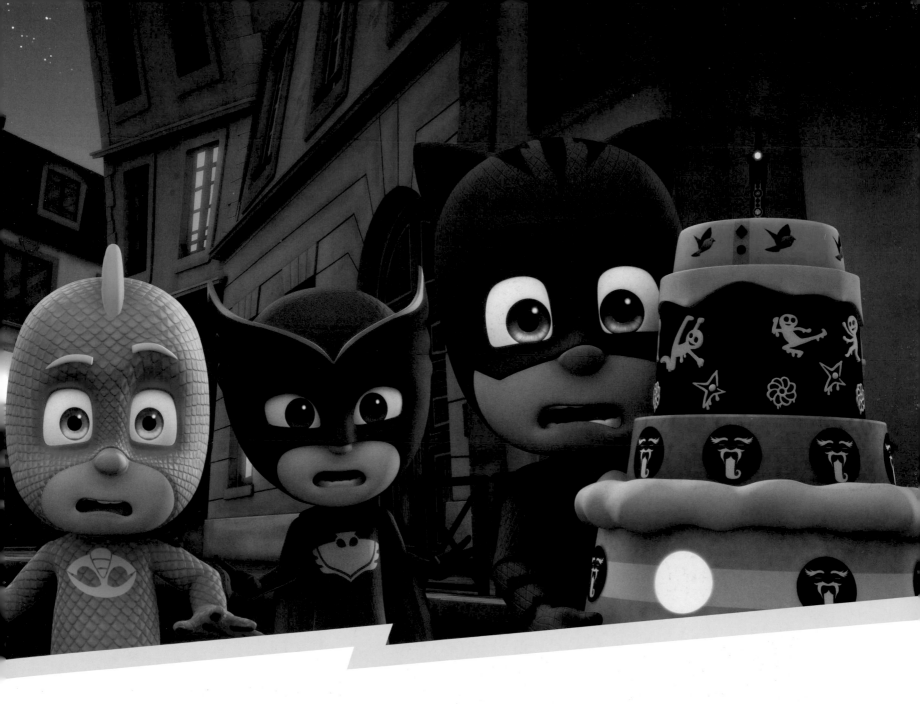

"What's going on?" asked Catboy.

Night Ninja sniggered. "When the last icing swirl turns blue, it will blow whipped cream everywhere. When everyone tries to clear it up, they'll get sticky-splat-stuck."

Night Ninja had landed the PJ Masks with a Sticky-Splat Whipped Cream Splatto Cake. It was a birthday disaster!
"That will teach you to try and spoil my party!" he shouted, disappearing out of sight.

Owlette frowned.
"If everyone gets stuck,"
she whispered, "no one will be able to come to Gekko's birthday party."
Catboy looked at Gekko's sad face.
He had made a big mistake.

"I'm sorry," said Catboy. "This is all my fault. But I have an idea how to put things right. It's time to be a hero!"

Gekko and Owlette punched the air.
The PJ Masks were back in action!

"Ha-ha!" bellowed Night Ninja. "I win!"

The baddie looked over his shoulder and spotted the Master Fang cake sitting on the backseat. A light flashed and the last icing swirl turned blue.

"Uh-oh."

The cake exploded, covering Night Ninja in icky-sticky cream! The baddie struggled out of the icky-sticky cake splat and ran away, taking his Ninjalinos with him.

SPLAT!

Catboy picked up the lizard cake and handed it back to Gekko. The hood closed on the Gekko-Mobile. When it lifted again, the vehicle had been auto-cleaned.

"Wow!" gasped Owlette.

Catboy grinned. "Do you think he'd let a cake explode in his Gekko-Mobile without auto-cleaning?"

The heroes laughed. Now Gekko was set for the best lizard birthday ever!

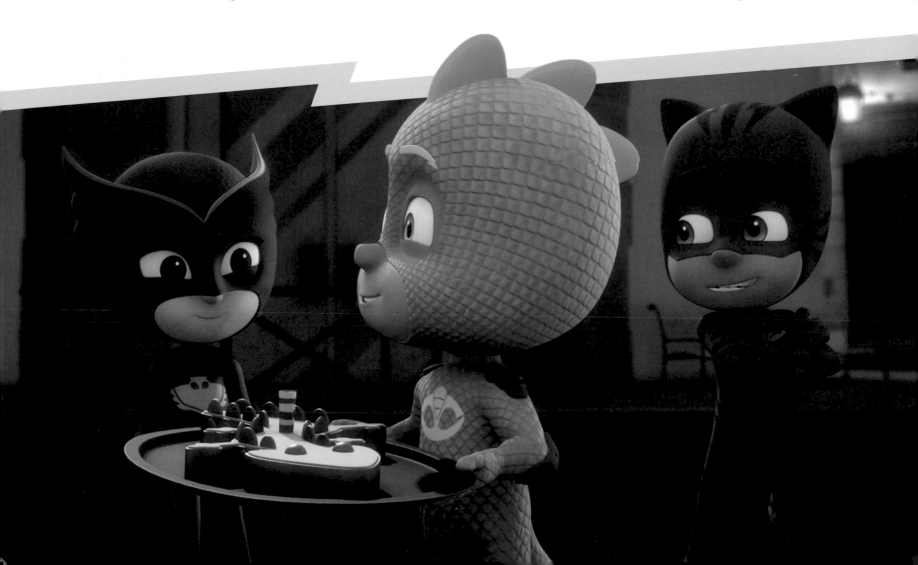

PJ MASKS ALL SHOUT HOORAY,
'CAUSE IN THE NIGHT WE SAVED THE DAY!